Passage

Orb Chronicles

K. D. Morey

This is a work of fiction. Names, characters, businesses, places, events and incidents are either the products of the author's imagination or used in a fictitious manner. Any resemblance to actual persons, living or dead, or actual events is purely coincidental.

Copyright © 2015 by K. D. Morey
All rights reserved. This book or any portion thereof may not be reproduced or used in any manner whatsoever without the express written permission of the publisher except for the use of brief quotations in a book review.

Edited by Trevor D. Richardson
Cover Illustration and Orb Symbol by K. D. Morey

Printed in the United States of America

First Printing, 2015

ISBN-13: 978-1514663073

ISBN-10: 1514663074

http://faeforge.wordpress.com/

We swear to seek. To know, to delve beyond the horizons set by the generations before us.

Books by K.D. Morey

The Orbs

Beautiful Machine

Promise Rising (coming soon)

Orb Chronicles

Passage

- 1 -

Bound and blinded, there was no going back. With his head swimming in stifling darkness and feet crunching onto sharp gravel, the only way out was forward. He stumbled and a jolt of pain lanced up his right leg. A larger rock on the path, of course there would be. The headmasters would be certain to place such a literal symbol of his progress, or lack thereof.

Kav spread his feet wide and gingerly prodded the ground ahead, his large toe catching the smooth lump of another stone. He extended his leg as far as he could, stretching his tail back for balance. His toes found gritty path again and his breath quickened with excitement. *Progress!* His breath steamed up the inside of his cowl, making it as hot as a Fintanin steam bath. Kav didn't care. More successful steps and he would be done, and this torment would be over.

What a sight he must be - each step an ungainly trip or desperate crouching search with feet or tail. Muffled titters told him exactly how he looked. A young Fintanin once told him that his people were tall, delicate, and regal. Kav chuckled to himself, *not right now friend, not right now.* He tried to imagine his postures as more of a dance and less of a botched mating display. But none of that mattered. All that mattered was the goal.

A deep dip, paired with overconfidence and he found himself falling forward. He tried to twist but only managed to speed his fall face first into the gravel. Teeth clacked and rattled his entire skull. This time outright laughter erupted all around him, the other students who came to watch, friends, foes, teachers, they all chuckled at his expense. All except one, his mother was out there somewhere, watching with her ocean blue eyes. She probably gasped but still stood tall, proud with her crest lifted high.

Kav struggled back to his feet, a little unsteady now thanks to a scrape on his knee. After a few more tentative steps he heard it. The opening lines from the oath of learning:

"We swear to seek. To know…"

He knew what that meant, the final part of the path had been reached. Each step was more confident now. Back straight, he strolled forward following the headmaster's deep clear baritone hum.

"…to delve beyond the horizons set by the generations before us."

Breathing deep, he tried to keep his excitement from showing. *This was it!* Twenty long years and his childhood and status as a dependent finally at an end. He was an adult and a citizen with a voice.

"Not for fame. Not for glory. But for the truth…"

One, maybe two more steps...

"May our path to the horizon be eternal."

Kav paused, his foot hovering in space. Students never knew what was on the path, they changed it for each graduate, as was too fitting, but something in the headmaster's tone told him to pause, to not trust his last step. Wasn't it the way of knowing? To not assume you have all the answers?

Centering his weight on his back leg he probed forward with his foot. Open air, a deep hole that would have collapsed him in a heap. He reached further and found the lip. With a heave, he crossed the gap and landed on the far side. Legs wide, tail straight behind, he froze there breathless and willed that he wouldn't tip backwards.

Even the very air seemed to hold its breath as he shifted his weight forward. A fall this far in would not only be an embarrassment but could even land him in another year or more of schooling. His people did not suffer impatient graduates among the educated elite. Taking a deep breath he dared to stand tall. Whistles erupted around him from his classmates and a hand touched the top of his cowl.

"We welcome you into the light of knowledge," intoned the headmaster, and the world was ablaze in sunlight.

***

Friends found him first. Jahco, with his laughing green eyes, slapped him on the back. Thelse blinked at him shyly from across the small gathering, her turquoise eyes almost made him forget where he was before the others gathered to offer their congratulations. He could feel the small cut dribbling blood from his knee. Kav didn't care, his joy was so immense he could almost feel it trying to burst through his skin.

"HA! Kav! That was bold! Leaping that pit! I thought you were doomed when I saw that but you surprised us all!" Jahco seemed as pleased as he was. Kaval felt more than a little guilty, he wondered if his friend would ever walk the path.

"Thank you," he struggled for more words but was halted when he spotted his mother across the grounds.

She stood with her arms folded over her chest, the deep grey skin of her arms marred with fading impressions from her fingers, the fringe of her lavender crest slowly relaxed from her earlier stress, yet her tail twitched in agitation.

The explanation stood in a cluster around her. Dwarfed by her willowy frame, they were small, smaller than Nilegi, but not by much. Their skins, however, were warm shades of pink or brown and their heads were thick with earth-toned manes. Like the Nilegi and Fintanin they had clear and over obvious genders.

Kaval gawked at them.

Jahco didn't miss his chance.

"Can you believe it!? It's the new species. What were they... Hucans? Hoolans?"

"Humans," Kaval gulped, no one told him dignitaries would be at his graduation, had he known he might have tripped after all.

"What do you think your mother is talking to them about?"

"I don't know."

"Look at how beady their eyes are. How do they see anything? Don't they remind you of a Fintanin but small and starved? Then again the Nilegi look like bleached, shaved, and starved Fintanin. Come to think of it, they have hair like a Fintanin, except for that one with the red mane. I wonder if I should dye mine red. What do you think?"

Kaval was lost, staring at the squat little mammals. It wasn't long ago when the humans first started showing up in the Orbs. News traveled fast and before long one or two humans were spotted walking the streets of Lonsara, the capitol of Susite, site of the planets largest ground gate, and center of Ailo civilization. Not to mention his home.

Then and now the Ailo seemed to make the visiting humans uncomfortable, as they were rarely seen outside their embassy. Naked curiosity and enthusiasm seemed unfortunately lost on them. But it had been three centuries since a new race appeared in the orbs. These newcomers should just understand that, shouldn't they?

"Kaval?"

"Yes?" he blinked and looked over at his friend.

"I asked, do you think they have business with your mother?"

Kav sighed, "Of course they do, why else?"

Jahco twisted his neck towards them and cocked his head to the side, "Which language are they speaking?"

All the students, himself included, had been encouraged to learn the three major human languages - a lyrical, a clipped, and an expressive. All major trade tongues. They spoke to each other and watched whatever media they could find from the humans for practice. Kav shook his head at his friend. Jahco had made a point of learning some language with the best insults, while ignoring the other three.

He cocked his head to the side, mirroring his friend, and listened, "English."

Jahco sighed and let his crest fall, "I never learned that one."

Kav patted Jahco's shoulder before breaking away towards the group. His heart pounded with each step. Finally, to look at a human up close, he couldn't help his crest lifting up in curiosity.

As he approached, he could see the sweat standing out on their brows. Heavy uniforms covered them from chin to toes. He snorted to himself. Who would wear winter protection in the middle of the Lonsaran summer? With the sisters shining their radiance from high overhead, the city was perfectly habitable and warm. His own people were not so burdened. Simple drapes of fabric and harnesses for personal items left them free to feel the fine air on their skin.

The aliens fidgeted, digging stubby fingers into their collars and keeping wary eyes on the other Ailo, who barely contained themselves around the strangers. Like Shavlee searching for scraps at the docks, they lurked just at the edge of social propriety. The headmaster had no such qualms. He strode up to the group and bowed low, letting his lengthy whiskers touch the ground.

Kaval slowed, letting them exchange introductions. The humans struggled with a formal greeting, calling the headmaster female on accident. Odds were they couldn't tell by looking. The headmaster tipped his head back and laughed, evoking nervous chuckles from the primates. Kav took his cue and stepped up next to his mother.

"Ah, and here is my son, Kaval," she said. Her voice spoke the human language with a beautiful sing-song tone that made their own clipped accents sound like a metronome.

He bowed, lower than the headmaster, letting his whiskers drag on the moss for a moment longer.

"Kaval, this is Liz VanVeen, head of the Earth Renew Project."

He looked up from the ground, keeping his back bent and the humans at eye level. The red-haired one stepped forward and returned a curt bow. Kav didn't take his eyes off... her? Her — the face was smooth and showed no whiskers, and her clothing bulged with telltale lumps. She was pinker than the rest and her tiny eyes were the same ocean blue as his own. He stretched his neck to peer deeper into her eyes and the human balked backwards a step.

Mother's hand was at his shoulder, "Kaval, the humans do not enjoy being scrutinized so."

Kav pulled back and stood tall, "Sorry mother, but she has the same color eyes as us."

She waved him away, "My apologies, VanVeen, you and your companions are the first humans my son has seen up close. Forgive his curiosity."

VanVeen's mouth twisted and her teeth showed. At first, Kav thought she was getting ready to attack, until he saw the corners of her eyes crinkle in a smile.

"It's quite all right, Ms. Ri'Lavanre. He's young, curious, and freshly graduated. You must be quite proud, both of you."

Kav turned his face away and swished his tail, embarrassed and quite pleased with the praise.

"Please, call me Telas. And yes, I am quite proud of him. Two decades is a record for one to finish the academy."

VanVeen's eyes went wide, "Rigorous."

"Rightfully so," Telas blinked in satisfaction.

Kav watched his mother share a look of mirth with the human. A look he was certain had something to do with him.

"Mother? I am pleased to meet them, but I have to ask. Why are they here?"

Telas chuckled. "I am to oversee the completion of their first terraformer, VanVeen here has been leading the project on Earth. YOU will be coming with us. We had only to wait for your graduation. You will assist me, consider it your first assignment."

Kav gulped. "What if I had tripped?"

"Then you would be staying here. And I might be looking for a different assistant."

"No pressure," he muttered.

VanVeen's smile broadened, "I think your mother knew you would succeed. She had nothing but praise for you, and if Telas trusts you so do I." She folded her arms leaving no room for argument.

As disconcerting as it was to watch the aliens face contort to her mood, Kav found it bizarrely endearing.

***

Over the next few days, Kav could hardly handle his mounting excitement. Not only would he be leaving the Academies that he had called home for the majority of his life, but he would be leaving his planet for the first time, traveling the Orbs and visiting an alien planet. As if that wasn't exciting enough, he would be one of the select few who would be allowed to visit a brand new world of the Orbs.

Keeping with tradition, he held a party that very night and gave away all but his most personal possessions. Keeping only a wrist computer, and a handful of cool weather drapes and grooming tools. As fun as it was, he found he spent most of the night out on the balcony staring at the summer stars and dreaming of his coming life as his friends hooted, drank, and smoked themselves into a stupor. Come dawn, his floor was a carpet of serpentine bodies, spindly limbs and tails, as the other young Ailo slept it off.

As he had prodded them awake, Kav wondered how much he would miss his friends, this city and its variety and wonder, the bath water seas, the flocks of shavlee, and the pillars of stone teeming with life dwarfing even the arcologies of Lonsara.

The following day, his hopes melted like morning dew. He visited the libraries to waste a little more time before his mother and VanVeen were ready to go.

Earth — he didn't expect his search to turn up much, but was instead bombarded by information. Similar climate, slightly heavier gravity, more and larger land masses, larger moon, and a single white sun, culture, music, entertainment, art, politics, wars - all of it was at his fingertips.

At his graduation, it struck him as odd that there was a terraformer system being built on an inhabited world, let alone a cradle world. The real answer slapped him in the face. For the past three centuries, a single Ailo lifetime, humanity had unwittingly destroyed their delicate biosphere. By the time their science had truly realized the impact of their actions it was already too late. Countless lost species, altered weather patterns, droughts, storms, and then the Orb opened and changed everything. There were rules set down by the Orb council, and no sentient species would be allowed to suffer when aid was available. A provision both his people and the Fintanin fought for so that no species should be held accountable for its isolated ignorance. It was still up to them to govern themselves, but if help was asked for, help was given.

Kav, with heavy heart, was headed to a disaster zone. His mother was an engineer advising their kind in the proper care and feeding of a terraformer in the hope that someday, far in the future their world would become more livable again.

Learning this, there would be no chance of sleep. Try as he might to view it as an adventure, all he could think of was the people he was going to be subjected to. What kind of beings would do such a thing? To ruin a world full of wonder, their *only* world at the time, for what? He couldn't even imagine a justifiable reason.

With insomnia on his shoulders, he embarked on one last swim and climb to the top of the largest sea stack in the bay.

The water was slick against his skin as he speared through the turquoise waves. Familiar stones greeted his hands as he clambered up the side of the stone in a tradition as old as the Ailo themselves.

At the top, he settled to his rump and looked out over the city, its bright lights and towers blending into the jungles around it. Ships lifted into the air heading for the Orb, and personal craft tacked against the star-studded sky. The night air was sweet with flowers that draped over the flanks of the pillars and the moon shone down with its liquid silver and blue orb gate. The smaller sub moons glittered like gems in a necklace.

It would be an adventure, one he hoped to survive.

***

Kav's sulking did not, could not, last long. Despite knowing what was coming, there was still the undeniable newness ahead. After twenty long years at the academy, it was time — even if the destination was less than desirable.

He arrived at the Earth embassy with nothing but a small pack slung over his narrow shoulders and a cup of a bitter beverage wrapped in his hands.

At first, he couldn't comprehend why the human staff lined up at the opportunistic little stand just off the embassy grounds. But there they were, right alongside a good number of Ailo who seemed adamant about getting their share, not exactly fighting for a place in line but defending it with many shifty glares and bristled crests. Then the smell hit him, it filled the air with a roasted almost caramel-scented steam, and he found his place in line behind a handsome elder riti.

The third-gendered Ailo swished her tail unconsciously as they waited.

It was a pleasant enough distraction as he stood in line and waited, and waited, and finally was rewarded with his own cup. Much to his disappointment, it was hot and black and tasted like burnt dirt. Still not wanting to waste it he sipped, trying to discover the attraction. By the time he found Liz and his mother overseeing the loading of supplies onto a bulky hov transport on the embassy grounds, Kav was a jittering wide-eyed mess.

His mother saw him first.

"Kav?" she rushed to him and placed a slender palm on the side of his neck. "Your pulse is high, what is wrong?"

"Nn-nn-Nothing!"

Liz was there a moment later, a look of deep concern creasing her face. She sniffed the air and took the empty cup from his hands, "Coffee?"

"Is that what this is called?"

VanVeen snorted and looked him up and down, barely having a chance to cover her mouth before she started to giggle.

"Your son is adorable, Telas."

"Is he going to be all right?" she asked, smoothing back his crest like he was an unruly infant again.

"Yeah," she wiggled the cup in front of his face. "You get this from the place outside?"

He nodded with a little more enthusiasm than he expected, making his teeth clack.

"He will be fine, maybe next time don't get so much?"

"Okay."

Kav felt stupid, some graduate he was.

Liz peered at him totally unable to suppress the sparkle of amusement in her eyes, "Is that all you are bringing? In that teeny, tiny, little back pack?"

Kav blinked, "Yes?"

Why was that so funny? He found himself adjusting the seat of the straps.

VanVeen smiled and said not another word before turning and leading them to the transport.

- 2 -

There were two ways to travel the Orbs. Each had their merits, each had their drawbacks.

An individual could pass through one of countless ground gates scattered across worlds known and unknown. Most civilizations monitored access, approving passage the same as someone might purchase a ticket for a skyliner. Once entered, each and every gate lead to the impossible geometry of the station known as the Orb. It existed nowhere, and everywhere, a nexus outside of physical space anchored into the sub-surface of countless moons. None had ever traveled all of its passages and attempts to map the internal gates always came up short. The relic of a people long vanished, often worshiped, and known only as the Makers.

Common routes were marked, areas of similar destination settled by the people who used it. Creating wards, like mini cities, pockets of their cradle worlds inside the Orb. This means of passage was easy and any species, even people devoid of space-flight let alone electricity or even the wheel, could pass with ease. This trek was longer but filled with the varied splendor of sentient life. Nilegi, straight-backed and pale, marched in their black uniforms, their skin glowing with fashionable implants, right past spear-wielding RaShak who glowered at every alien they could see with their beady reptilian eyes. Gold-decked Fintanin priests, masked and aloof Metharom, tiny Liton, squat Dara, terrified Humans, and even the occasional hulking form of a Xueria, and more and stranger, all of them were there, trading and traveling and generally being amazing. The Orbs were the greatest blessing to civilization in all of collected history.

Then there was the other route, the boring route, the route they were taking. Kav slouched deeper into his seat and crossed his arms as he watched the vast blue jewel of Susite grow ever smaller.

Burdened with supplies, and a great many of them to boot, a ship through the lunar gate was the only sane way to go. Aside from the simple logistics of hauling that much equipment, any large packages would draw the attention of thieves who would take the opportunity to grab what they wanted and dive through the nearest ground gate. Despite this, those not so fortunate to have mastered the skies and basic space travel sent caravans through, complete with armed guards risking their supplies and sometimes their lives for the chance to trade with all known civilizations. It wasn't as if the Orbs were uncivilized, the council maintained a police force large enough to rival some armies, but they were not omniscient and couldn't be everywhere all the time.

Their transport drew closer to the small silver moon, its pocked surface and looming captured asteroids not nearly as artistic this close. He sighed, blowing his whiskers out like streamers. The cough-ee was wearing off along with his enthusiasm. It was real now, he was off his planet.

Liz or VanVeen or whatever he was supposed to call the red-haired human sat across from him. Whenever she wasn't watching home... no, the *alien* world, vanish into the distance, she would steal glances at him, always with the same twist of the lips he had come to understand as amusement.

"So your mother tells me you studied physics?"

He yanked his awareness back from the edge of a doze with a snort.

"Sorry, I didn't realize you were..."

"Tired?" Kav sat up and rubbed his face with both hands. He leaned forward and rested his elbows on his knees. "No need to apologize, I should stay awake."

She nodded, letting the silence stretch, "So?"

"So?"

"Did you study physics?"

"Oh... right, right." Kav sat back and folded his arms again, making a point to sit straighter than before despite the discomfort to his tail, "I did, and engineering, among other things. At the academies we have to learn a little of everything. We don't have to do well at things outside our focus, but at least come to appreciate their complexities if they are beyond us.

Innovation, creativity, and knowledge are what we value. Understanding connectedness is what keeps a mind flexible. Our first three years are all just to see what we might be good at."

Liz cocked her head to the side in a very Ailo expression of curiosity, "Did you expect the focus you got?"

He scoffed, "Yes and no. I mean I ended up with all the right criteria. But…"

"But what?"

With a sigh, he gazed back out the window, "Our interstellar ships always need good crews. But, as it turns out, I had a better mind for theory and less for application, better for engine design and labs, not so much for field work. So, despite my mixed focus, I couldn't qualify. Not yet anyway. It doesn't mean I will only and ever be a physicist and engineer helping my mother out, it's just where I will start. So they say anyway."

"You don't sound so sure."

"Eh… I did well with all the required sub focuses - propulsion, materials, entanglement, and so on. But the headmasters have the final say. Perhaps, someday, I will get to be on a ship."

Liz shook her head, "I don't blame you. Your people are the only ones I know of who even have interstellar ships. To serve on something like that…"

He dismissed the praise with a wave, "Don't get too in awe, we went to one, maybe two other stars before our Orb gate opened. After that, my people decided what we had was good enough."

She frowned. Before she could continue, Kav gasped. She turned and looked out the windows. The Orb gate was before them, enormous, like flying into a blue sun. They both forgot the conversation as the ship passed into the gate meniscus.

***

Arches of white metal vaulted into the distance and lights glowed along every surface of the tunnel, a networked maze of impossibly large corridors spreading off into infinity. It was immediately clear to him that the network was not housed inside the moon or even reality. Kav had studied some of the theory of the Orb's in the academy, but it was wholly different to see it. The scale was brain-breaking.

Liz helped soothe him by looking as awed as he felt, mouth hanging open and eyes wide. He expected the head of a project like hers would be a little more jaded. Instead, she ogled at a formation of sleek black Nilegi ships as they zipped past so close that their running lights bathed their seats in amber-red light. And, like him, she gasped when they passed another tunnel and the massive shape of an Ailo interstellar ship loomed in the space. It dwarfed all the other transports like a hucha sky beast surrounded by shavlee.

"Is that?" Liz kept her gaze glued to the ship.

"It is. *Promise*, most likely on its way back from one of our expanded colonies."

"Incredible," she breathed.

He felt the pang of regret, but let it pass as they watched the great ship vanish from sight.

***

Another meniscus and they were in the true void of space once again. A different blue jewel sat perfect in the distance. They watched in silence for a long time as the dot drew closer.

Liz's bright mood dimmed with each passing moment and Kav found he couldn't contain his curiosity any longer.

"What is wrong? Aren't you happy to see home?"

She looked at him with moist eyes, "I am, but..."

"But what?"

With a sigh, she sat back from the window, "I've been on your world for a month now, arranging supplies and making final plans." She looked away, "Your world is so beautiful, clean, full of life. The capitol makes me think of what Indonesia must have been like... before."

Kav grunted, he didn't feel the need to finish her sentence. He stroked his whiskers, as short and adolescent as they were, "It wasn't always that way. Our planet too had its dark days, it is part of the reason why we pushed into space so early, how we know so much about terraforming, and why the academies are so important. The only way out is forward."

She smiled, "It's good to know recovery is possible, if I didn't have that hope I might not have had the will to even be on this project. Still... I won't get to see it in my lifetime."

"Why not?"

"I'm thirty and it will be at least a century before any real changes. I will be gone by then."

Kav blinked, "You... such a short time?"

"Yes, I know, your kind live three times as long as we do. I envy you, you can come back here someday and tell my great-grandchildren what Earth was like, and you will get to see the results of all this hard work."

He opened his mouth and shut it twice before reaching forward to place his hand over hers, the long dusty grey digits dwarfing her little pink fingers. When he looked up into her eyes the tears were flowing, a trait they shared as a species.

There was nothing else he could do. What could he even say? Agree? It was the truth. Give her meaningless platitudes? She would know them as false as much as he would. Congratulate her far-minded thinking? Would that matter to a human? Even if it did, it was an empty victory for her.

She nodded mutely and withdrew her hand. Silently, he cursed the overthinking that left him speechless when someone needed him.

***

Their ship neared the world and the surface was a blanket of white. Far to the left, in the deep sea of clouds, a central eye punctured the shroud over the ocean. Soon the entire world was nothing but swirling mist. The winds buffeted the ship, trying to toss it down like a broken toy. Kav could hear the whine of the grav engines adjusting to the shifting currents. The storm itself was far away, but thunderheads heavy with rain still covered their destination.

When the ship touched ground, Kav was startled to hear the soft patter of rain and the breath of wind. It was hard to tell the time of day, clouds blanketed everything in perpetual dusk.

"Is this normal?"

"For California?" she shook her head and chuckled. "No, far from it, dry as a bone, but that hurricane out in the South Pacific is kicking up all kinds of water. I heard reports of landslides all through the region. Areas not already evacuated thanks to the rising seas have been evacuated thanks to the mud."

"Are we safe?"

"Yeah, this is one of the few stable areas."

His mother passed through their cabin, "They are waiting. Come, we need to clear customs."

Outside, the warm rain pattered his skin. It felt greasy and thick and went well with the bogged down feeling in his legs. Their gravity was only a little higher than home, but it was enough to notice.

They were walking across a field of concrete painted with bright yellow lines. Other ships sat all around them, Ailo and Nilegi next to the more clunky human-made ships. Far in the distance, he could see a tall linked fence topped in wicked spirals of wire. Armed guards pushed back a crowd of humans on the other side.

Kav found himself slowing. The humans were jumping and screaming, holding large white signs while they ignored the rain. When he trailed behind, the crowd became even more animated as they held the signs high overhead where he could see.

"Welcome space brothers?" Kav read the words out loud.

Liz was at his elbow, pulling him along, "Come on."

"But... what are they doing?"

"Fans."

"Fans?"

"It's been only ten years, there are still a lot of humans who are excited you exist."

"Me?"

"Well, no, not you personally, but all alien life."

"Wow."

In all the excitement he hadn't stopped to contemplate how incredible it would be to learn about worlds beyond your own for the first time. The excitement he felt had to be only a fraction of what they did.

"Why can't they come in?" he asked.

Liz laughed, "Because for every one of them there is another human who would rather you didn't exist."

He felt himself bristle, "Oh, well, let's not meet any of them."

She chuckled and led him with the others towards a sprawling series of pre-fab buildings. The 'fans' were out of sight now, but another cluster of humans waited just behind another fence close to the door his mother ducked through. This group held black devices on their shoulders and giant flood lamps.

As they neared, one pressed on the fence and shouted a series of questions at him so fast he barely understood them.

"Excuse me! Can you tell us about the progress on the terraformers? How have your people felt about the trade? Is it true that the Ayh-lee-oh consider humanity in their debt and that you have requisitioned parts of Earth for yourselves? What are your people's plans for Earth?"

Kav stood wide-eyed as he gripped the straps of his tiny backpack. They were a writhing sea of questions, when one stopped talking another started, and on and on.

They were all soggy and a whiff of strong perfume caught his nose. Kav sneezed and the entire mass rocked back as if he had just hosed them down with a plasma torch. He was too far to have even hurt them, let alone catch them in his sneeze. They had to know the protocols all species had to go through to ensure no cross-contamination or other biological hazards would get passed. They had to know he was safe to be here... didn't they? Liz was at his elbow again, dragging him away from the crowd.

"Ugh, reporters. Sorry, I should have warned you about that."

"Why were they asking all those questions? None of that is true, we are just following Orb protocol. And as far as I know, humanity traded plenty of their own technology for our help."

"The press likes to make up stuff to make their stories more exciting."

"They lie to the people?" Kav's eyes couldn't bulge any further.

"No they kind of just stretch the truth to the point of breaking," one glance at Kav stopped her, "Ok, yeah they lie."

"But I'm just a.... teenager? Is that the word? How would I know anything?"

"How old are you?"

"Same as you, three decades."

Liz rolled her eyes.

"Adult or not, you aren't human and that is enough for them. Come on. We have a lot of crap to do before we all get to sleep and prepare for the trip to the worksite."

Liz took him deeper into the compound, ducking through endless halls, answering questions and letting serious looking men paw through his scant belongings. Eventually, they met with another Ailo who led them to a small side building where the ceilings were higher and there were beds long enough for them to rest on.

Kav felt exhaustion crush him only moments after laying his head on an overstuffed pillow.

***

The next morning, they broke their fast on fruits and flakey breads so sweet they made his tongue curl. They dined alongside the riti who had been named ambassadorial assistant assigned to this region.

Mother chatted with her as if they were old friends, catching the other Ailo up on news from home. The "embassy," as they were calling it, was just one of a cluster of prefab buildings housing the assistant staff from the other races who chose to help and trade with the humans.

He half-listened as they discussed plans.

"We have thought about helping them build arcologies as they lay plans for newer, more updated cities."

"It's a big project, do they have the stamina?"

"Only time will tell, Telas. Already I know they have brokered for a handful of small colonies to ease the population burden off world."

"Some will fight…"

"They always do…"

Liz burst in at that moment, weather-beaten and jerky with irritation. The tiny human dropped a pad on the table between the chatting Ailo.

"Can you believe this! Telas! Your son!"

Kav stretched his neck out and spied an article with his picture, mid-sneeze, a headline reading, "Ailo plague?"

He snarled, "It was perfume!"

The acting ambassador was unruffled, "I see they never get tired of *that* story."

Liz blinked and picked up her pad, "They've run this before?"

The riti bobbed her head, "Hmmm…Yes, two or three times at least."

"It's an outrage."

The two older Ailo shrugged, "Could be worse. Your people haven't done what the Nilegi did at first contact."

Kav swallowed hard, knowing what was coming next.

Liz took the bait, "Why? What did they do?"

The riti smoothed her whiskers and squinted in a smile, "Total war until one way of thinking came out on top. The Nilegi Imperium was born when their gates opened and bathed their world in blood. Haven't they taught you anything? That is why your people are trading with us now instead of the Nilegi. Despite a cosmetic similarity, your leaders found them far too brutal."

"No… I didn't know. I'm just an engineer, not a politician."

"Oh," The riti purred, "you are now, my dear, you are now."

- 3 -

They said their goodbyes and made their way back to the transport, now armed with all the proper clearances to enter Earth's airspace unopposed. The ship glided over the clouds, heading north. The white blanket was interspersed with towers of violent clouds, dark, bruise-grey and heavy with rain.

The others said nothing as they watched the clouds roll past. Kav wondered what lurked beneath the heavy cloud cover. Blighted landscape? Mud washed hills? Or were they out over the ocean already? His wish was soon answered as the transport angled down with a lurch. It punctured the clouds to glide over the roiling crests of grey water. To his right, Kav could see muddy brown hills dotted with toppled buildings growing more dilapidated with each passing moment as more water poured down from the sky.

A tap on the shoulder pulled his attention from the sad remains of whatever city clung to the shore. Looking forward, he quickly saw why Liz had tapped him.

The terraformer tower was huge. One of dozens like it around the planet. Its roots sank deep into the churning waves and concrete reached to scrape the belly of the clouds. Its sides sloped upward to a narrow funnel up top. Stable, plain, and built to last. He had read of them, but had never seen one. And still had yet to see one complete. Scaffolding strained against the wind and clung to the outside of the structure. Even though it was built to be temporary, the scaffolds were still durable enough and large enough to land a transport, or three, right alongside the housing for the army of workers who had built the thing.

The major labor and construction having been complete, most of the housing now stood dark. The teams of biologists, biochemists, environmental engineers, and physicists were next, some on staff already some on the way. These people, who would ignite the engines and begin the slow process of stabilizing the atmospheric gasses and, ergo, the climate, people like them.

The transport landed with a soft thud on the platform and they all held their breath as the sounds of creaking scaffold echoed through the hull. Engines powered down, systems turned off and the weight of the vehicle committed fully to the landing pad. In the absence of engines, the sounds of wind and heavy rain only accentuated the gentle rhythmic creaking of the scaffolds. They hardly had the chance to breathe a sigh of relief before the hatches opened and humans wrapped in layers of rain gear ushered them out across the platform.

Liz took the lead, running with head down towards the double doors of the labs. Kav and his mother both stood tall in the pouring rain, stretching their necks and shoulders before ambling after her. Too much time in tiny rooms was already giving his young spine an aching knot. Luckily for them, the ceilings in the labs were quite high and, after ducking the door, they both stood tall again and gave their soaking crests a vigorous shake.

Once the water was out of his face, Kav could finally give the room a serious look. Dozens of beady human eyes focused on them, their expressions a dazzling mix of fear and wonder. An older male with grey streaks in his hair broke the stillness first by walking over to Liz and wrapping her in his arms.

"How was Susite?"

The man's deep baritone surprised Kav for coming from such a small creature. He found himself dipping his head to their level to hear better.

Liz stepped back and shot a glance to the Ailo, "It was good, amazing actually. Dutch, this is Telas, one of their top civil and environmental engineers." She gestured at his mother who bowed gracefully to the man, "And her son, Kaval, a recent graduate from their academies, a physicist and engineer."

Kav blinked and dipped even lower into an awkward bow before snapping back up to his full height.

A new look washed across the older human's face - suspicion. He said, "I thought that we were all clear to start final ignition?"

Telas stepped forward and folded her long, graceful arms, "Almost. I am here for final inspection, ignition done without it could lead to disaster."

"But we already started some of the base groundwork on the seabed," Dutch folded his arms, mimicking the tall Ailo woman.

"Then it will have to go on pause..."

Groans sounded around the room as the spell their presence had cast over the scientists finally broke. Kav sympathized, no one liked being told what to do or that they had to wait to get work done. They turned back to their tables.

Damn aliens ordering us around...
That kid better not get in the way...
Did there have to be two of them?

These and worse remarks were muttered under coffee-soured breath.

"Show me the way, Mr. Dutch," his mother's sing-song broke him from his own swirling doubts.

The man nodded to her and led Telas away into the compound, leaving Kav to shift foot to foot in a room full of people that hated him.

Liz came to his rescue, "Here let me show you where to put your things. We can't get any work done until all the supplies are offloaded anyway."

She tugged his elbow and encouraged his lethargic feet to move. Eyes followed them through the room. Kav had never felt so gangly and out of place in his life, not even the time he had asked to join Thelse in her bed for the night. Memories of that evening were about all he had to keep him warm right now.

He stooped his head so he wouldn't feel so tall, maybe the humans wouldn't sneer if he wasn't towering over them. He kept his tail from moving so they wouldn't notice and he felt his crest go flat against his head and neck. Anything, anything at all to help. He had no idea if it worked since he refused to meet their gaze.

Liz whispered, "Don't worry, they are all just stressed, tired, and want this project finished. Your timing is just terrible is all. Once they can get back on track they will warm up to you. Doesn't help that most of them have never seen an alien in person before today either."

Kav could only snort as the glares hammered his bent and retreating back.

***

The following day, Kav tried to find something to do. Anything to help. His mother was somewhere deep in the guts of the facility and, despite his own expertise, he had no idea where to even begin. Everyone here had their own system, their own rhythm, and he was a discordant bleat in the choir.

He didn't even know where the power system was hiding or what he would do with it if he found it.

So, failing everything else, he found himself wandering a vast chamber in the labs filled with clear tanks of green tendrils floating in water.

Guessing it was some kind of aquatic plant he bent over a tank and peered at the waving green fronds. A human male worked nearby with his arms elbow deep in the water. Kav gave him a respectful nod while the man pretended to ignore him.

The fronds were marred with regularly spaced pods of some kind, but they looked clear. Full of air? Kav reached out a slender finger and prodded the air sack with a claw. It bobbled in the water. It *was* full of air! Kav felt his crest lift as he reached again to prod it, watching it bob much to his delight.

"Don't touch that!"

Kav snatched his hand back and cradled it like it had been bitten. Resigned, he stepped back from the tank and squared up his shoulders.

"What is it?"

The man snorted, "Kelp."

"Kelt?"

"Kelp! Kel-P!"

"Kel-Ph"

"Close enough," he turned back to his work.

Uncertain, he twitched his tail and tried to walk away, but then he noticed what the man was doing. He moved with the swiftness of focused practice, grabbing each bundle of plants and dividing them before plunging their roots back into the strata. Each movement was the same, absolute perfection. Amazed,

Kav peered over the man's shoulder. His height afforded him a perfect view. He thought to ask but figured the purpose would reveal itself in time.

The man sighed and ducked under Kav's neck.

He followed, keeping his eyes glued to the human's hands. His movements slowed, then stopped. Kav blinked and looked down, meeting the man's squinted brown eyes.

"Please," Kav gestured to the tanks, "continue."

He ducked away from him again and stepped back with his hands up, "Just… get away from me!"

Before Kav could even form a response, the man stomped out of the room, leaving Kav to swallow his own bile. He didn't understand what had happened, or why the man was upset, but knew it wasn't good.

***

Rain pelted the window and the sea outside was as dark and turbulent as his mood. Kav felt deflated. He lay on the cot, his limbs wilted over the sides, chin resting on the edge as he gazed out the windows. One day, one lousy day, and he had already managed to cause an incident.

When he came out of the labs, his fear weighing down his steps more than the gravity, Dutch had scolded him, asking him to leave his crew alone. With no other options, he retreated to the rooms he shared with his mother and collapsed.

He didn't know how long he had laid there before he heard a gentle knock at the door.

"Can I come in?"

Kav sighed, feeling himself deflate a little bit more, "Yes, come in, Liz."

She opened the door, bathing the room in light for a moment before closing it to darkness again. He felt her weight settle by his hip as her hand found his shoulder.

"I heard what happened. Don't worry, it won't happen again. I've told them to cool it and let you help out."

"No."

"No?"

"It was my fault, Liz. I should have known better. I'm stupid."

She chuckled, "No, you are young. I tried to explain that to them. How your people are. Most of them got it… but…"

"But?"

Liz sighed, "None of this is your fault, but it's more than you being young, and more than you getting in the way or watching them. You have to remember you are a big weird alien to them. An observer watching their every move. You think you are just being curious. And you *are*, but they don't see that. They see a bizarre, expressionless, alien monster with no care for us beyond morbid curiosity."

"But I just want to understand, help, that's what I am here for. I don't judge."

"I know that, Kav," she smoothed his crest, pausing for a moment to run the thin feathery strands between her fingertips, "but they don't. Remember this is a first for most of them, not just their first Ailo, but their first alien."

"But the Nilegi…"

"Are way closer to us when it comes to how they communicate, their facial expressions, their sense of modesty and personal space. That's why we traded with them first and why it took ten years before we could handle your people."

He rolled to his side and looked up at her. It was dim, but he could make out her concerned smile. Kav asked, "What can I do then?"

"Be seen, but stay back. Let them work. If they invite you to help, then help, until then let them just get used to you being here. In time they will calm down."

He nodded, "tomorrow."

She ruffled his crest, "tomorrow then," with a pat she left him to mull over her words.

***

Liz was right. Over the next couple days the humans relaxed, glares turned from anger, to irritation, to simple curiosity as he ventured forth into their company. He toured the entire facility getting to see the marvels from the deep steam tunnels leading to the mainland to the top of the cooling tower. Most of the time he managed to keep his curiosity in check and when that failed he kept a wary eye on their mood, pulling back once they showed any signs of discomfort at his presence. He still didn't have the spine to engage them in any conversation, but his back straightened and his eyes brightened as he watched the people work to save their world.

The real work of bridging the gap was solely on his mother's capable shoulders. After dark, she would sit with them, eat their food, drink their booze and ignore their haunted looks to tell them jokes or talk about the impressive work they had done so far while the wind howled outside. Some of the jokes were crude to the point of tears and many were at his expense. Kav didn't mind, for every anecdote about her only son's shy and awkward life their acceptance of him grew a little more. He even learned a new phrase from them that confused him — "TMI," they would say, meaning "too much information." The concept was utterly foreign to him and his mother both, but it seemed to be a source of great humor to the humans so they shrugged their narrow shoulders and went along with it. He wished he had the guts to be like her, but every time he opened his mouth nothing but a weak little squeak would come out.

This night was like the others. Several of the humans near Telas were gasping for breath as she sipped at something called "whiskey." Kav had already tried it and found it made his whiskers stand on end. The mess hall was full as they gathered to hear his mother recount her courtship with the male and riti who would aid in his own conception. The subject of Ailo reproduction evidently fascinated the bi-gendered humans. He hoped it was because a few were biologists.

"His father was awkward just like him, so much so that when I mentioned we might bond in trinity he gagged on his lunch. His riti just laughed, she was amazing when she laughed, she liked the idea, neither one of them had thought about family and had no intention of raising one. I was already high in the civil engineering tiers and my extended family looked forward to seeing if I would. I liked them both, very creative, it was a good match."

Kav knew both his other parents in passing. His father had told him stories of other worlds and set his mind to looking for the horizon. His riti loved to take him climbing, a passion he still retained.

"So it takes three?" one of the humans leaned forward.

Telas blinked, "Yes, of course."

The man opened his mouth to ask another question when the doors swung open. Liz stomped in, covered head to toe in heavy rain gear.

"Whelp, I got bad news, everyone. Weather service just informed me that hurricane Polo has changed course and is heading this way. We are going to be stuck out here for a week or more."

A chorus of groans met her declaration. Dutch piped up, "Can't we take the shuttles out?"

"We can, but I don't want to leave a multimillion dollar project just sitting out here unguarded. Some of you will be going, the rest are stuck here. I will allow volunteers, of course, for either."

More grumbles until Telas's musical voice carried through the room. "I intend to stay," she contemplated her glass until she was certain she had their attention. "Do not worry. My inspections found the entire structure to be sound, even the scaffolds we sit on could weather a thousand storms."

"Glad to hear it," Liz shook off her coat, scattering puddles of water all over the floor, "because we need to be sleeping on that for a while."

"In that case, I hope you have enough supplies."

"Of course, we keep rations, water, you name it…"

"Whiskey to last the week? Because it sounds like we won't be getting any work done."

Laughter, enough to challenge the raging storm.

- 4 -

The storm answered in kind. The wind screamed and the windows shook from the gusts, but the structure stayed strong. Everything on the decks had to be hauled inside. The transports were sent away with as many people who wanted to go, leaving the pad empty. A skeleton crew was left to man the tower, Telas and Kav remained to suffer right alongside them.

It didn't take long for the sense of isolation to dampen their spirits. Even their evenings drawled on with everyone retreating into their cups. Kav found himself wishing he had stayed home or even failed his graduation. The monotony of rain, surf and wind threatened to drive him into a coma.

With his head resting on folded arms, Liz's fingers found their way into his crest. His eye swiveled to her and he could sense the care in her touch. There was nothing speaking of desire. Just one living being seeking to comfort and be comforted by the presence of another. Kav sighed and pushed his head under her hand so she could scratch behind his jaw. She giggled like a girl with a new pet as he let satisfaction rumble through his throat. It was something to keep his mind off things. Even if it did make him wish she was an Ailo for a moment.

The sound of a grav engine cutting through the storm didn't raise their listless spirits. But the noise of a concussive force jerked them out of their stupor a moment too late as the doors of the mess hall shattered open.

"Get down all of you! On your knees! DO IT NOW!" the man's scream stunned them, most of the room blinked in disbelief until the armed thugs grabbed their nearest victims and tossed them to the floor.

Telas stood, overturning a table, and a shot fired over her shoulder into the ceiling tiles.

"I'm not kidding, E.T. Get the fuck down!"

Telas dropped to her knees and held her hands in the air.

Kav's heart skipped a beat as he slithered down to the floor next to Liz.

"Wha…" but Liz's hand snaked over his mouth and held firm.

"Boss, isn't there supposed to be two of them?"

"Yeah, there is. Spill it alien, where is the other one?"

Kav felt his pulse hammer in his temples. He was still in shock, going from boredom to shots fired was not quite the thrill he was looking for.

Before he could even form another cohesive thought, the table they hid under skidded to the side and a solid hand grabbed him under the jaw, hauling him to his feet.

They may not have been tall enough to be imposing, but the vice-like grip still held him in check as he squirmed to find his feet.

"Got it!"

"Okay, everyone, on your feet. Outside. NOW!"

"What! Why are you…"

The man holding him back-handed Liz, sending her spinning to the ground, "No questions!"

Another man hauled her to her feet and pushed her in front of him. Guns trained on their backs as they were marched outside. Kav spared a glance to his mother, but her expression was unreadable, even to him.

On the pad, water pelted them, soaking them to the bone. A lone transport waited for them, grav engines holding it aloft in the wind. Confusion and terror reigned over the scientists.

As they approached the railing, their leader shouted over the maelstrom, "Toss the woman and the others, we got what we came for."

Liz's captor nodded once and shoved her face first over the railing. Her scream was snatched by the wind.

Everything froze — the wind, the men, the rain, even his heart. Never in his short life had Kav ever seen anything so callous. A voice cut into his thoughts, a voice he had heard since before his birth.

"Go... go now!"

He saw his mother's ocean eyes and her unmoving mouth, and before he could count or think he was moving.

The armed men were laughing, the scientists were screaming, and Kav was running. Despite the water on the deck and the heavy gravity pulling him down, his long limbs carried him past half of their captors before they could react. Shots rang out behind him. He didn't have a plan or even a prayer, all he could do was run and hope he could outrun his own terror.

Kav was at the railing, pushing the man over with him as he dove. His long lean body was like a spear speeding toward the seething water, just like he had done a thousand times from the spires of Lonsaran. Kav pushed away from the man, letting him spin behind him. He could see her twisting in the air, flame-colored hair a halo around her head against the dark water.

The physics were all wrong, he would never catch up to her. He just prayed the water was choppy enough not to crush her on impact. She vanished into the water as it crested and he lanced into the waves a second later.

Thick, oily water tugged at his limbs as he righted himself below the waves. Nictitating membranes covered his huge eyes as they dilated in the murky depths. No longer gangly, he moved with sinuous grace searching for the sinking woman.

Then he caught a glimpse of her fire hair sinking like a stone in the water. Kav twisted after her, catching her wrists and looping them over his neck. He didn't dare surface, not yet, not with them watching overhead. The man who shoved her sank past them, unconscious. Kav didn't spare him another thought as he moved with the water, trying to put the drowning man behind him.

***

The water seethed, grabbing him with angry hands and pushing him closer to the shore. As he neared what passed for dry land, he could see the shapes of buildings looming below, growing closer to his feet with each passing minute. Then it was silt and mud and tangled sticks. More than once, he had to dive to avoid snares in the water.

Finally, after what seemed an eternity of water, he spotted a sheltered inlet where the waves didn't dash on rock with bone-breaking force. Letting the current carry him, he corrected to wash into the muddy beach and hauled his exhausted limbs and Liz up behind him.

Kav rolled her off his back onto solid ground and lay on his belly next to her to take several deep breaths. His species was made to handle water, were born in water, but could not live in it. It seemed that humans were not so blessed. Liz lay still, her eyes closed under the mud.

Panic seized him for a moment before he leaned down and touched her face. It was cool but not cold. Deft fingers found a lazy pulse on her neck. He didn't have much time, he prayed their physiology wasn't too far off from the familiar.

The shirt had to go, he tore it open as a dim part of his mind marveled at the fluid dynamics of mammalian breasts. Fingertips searched her ribs, finding enough similar bones to feel safe to try. It was better than nothing, the alternative was to let her die. He thumped her sternum, gently, then harder, a third time he slammed his fist and she convulsed, rolling over to her side to vomit up gobs of muddy water. Her intake of breath wheezed and she vomited the full contents of her stomach onto the beach. With his hand on her shoulder, he kept her steady as she purged herself of the storm.

Wracking coughs were like music to his ears. She was alive.

"Where?" she croaked.

"They pushed you. That bastard pushed you," he had to shout over the storm. "We need to get under cover. Can you walk?"

Liz sat up and dropped back instantly, "No, my leg feels broken."

Kav hung his head and sighed. Of course it was broken. He stared down at his hands flexing his fingers in frustration. Glancing up he saw that Liz was still collapsed catching her breath. Each harsh wheeze made her fatty bits shift. On impulse he reached out a tentative finger poked her in the left breast. It wobbled just like the kelp.

Liz blinked, looked at her chest then back at Kav. Her hoarse chuckle grew into the kind of laughter you can only achieve when cheating death. Gut wrenching, hysterical, grateful to be alive insanity. Kav was caught up in it and soon both were doubled over howling along with the wind. Even as he hauled her to her good leg and crouched under her armpit they still snickered through every exhausted muscle and jolted bone.

***

Two figures struggled across the rocky landscape, fallen trees still writhing in the wind. Their goal was a concrete structure perched on top of a hill, the only sanctuary in the torn landscape. Legs ached, muscles complained, and yet they struggled on. The difference in their heights and gates made it impossible for them to travel with ease across the terrain, leaving Kav with an ache in his back that made him feel four hundred years old.

Kav eventually gave in and lifted Liz into his arms. Ailo were no stronger than a human but, luckily for him, Liz was small. Still, her dense little body surprised him. He stumbled and she gasped expecting them to crash into the rocks and jolt her already throbbing leg, but he kept his footing and slogged on. The gravity was grinding him to dust. It seemed so minor at first, just the difference of carrying a couple stones, but this was a burden he could no more set down than the woman in his arms.

They had been lucky to wash up in such a stony area. Elsewhere, mudslides had reduced the hills to ruins. But here the ground stayed firm. Kav couldn't see what was left of the city between the storm and full night descending over them.

Leaning Liz on the wall of the structure, Kav found a metal door and wrenched it open. A long dark hallway yawned before him, musty but dry. It would do. Scooping her back into his arms, he stalked down the hall into their dubious shelter.

The door swung closed behind him. Springs, he told himself. It was just springs. He blinked, waiting for his eyes to adjust to the darkness. He was no Nilegi, he wasn't made for the night. All he could see was that there was light down here.

"Can you see?" Liz whispered.

"Hmmm… not so much, you?"

"A dim light from… something?"

They groped forward like plants growing toward the suns, Liz reaching out from Kav's arms to guide him along the walls. Kav felt like he was right back at his test, shuffling his feet and prodding the ground ahead with each step before committing his weight.

They stepped out under a pool of light, the last luminance from dusk filtered down through a skylight. A branch had found the glass and punched a hole clean through, allowing a steady drip of water into the room.

If there were more skylights Kav couldn't see them. The room was huge and filled with the shattered remains of wooden furniture. Vibrant graffiti glowed in the gloom along the far walls.

Gingerly, Kav set Liz down on a dry patch of floor. Doing everything he could to not jostle her leg. She grunted in pain but otherwise gave no complaint.

Liz glanced around the room and swept her muddy hair out of her eyes, "Now what?"

He stood tall, letting the stretch reach from crest to tail tip, all the muscles of his back screamed then went lax as he pulled the exhaustion from his shoulders. With a shudder, he relaxed his arms and glanced down at his wrist. The computer was fried, no messages would be getting out from that thing.

With a sigh, he yanked it off and tossed it into her lap and rubbed his wrist. "Well, we need heat. There isn't a damn thing we can do until first light."

He gazed around the room taking in the broken wood. It was dry, they just needed a spark…

"Kav….?"

He snapped his focus back to Liz, "Yes?"

"You're shaking. You okay? Cold?"

"My people are pretty tolerant of temp…." he had lifted his hand, all of his four jointed fingers trembled violently, he was not cold.

He closed a loose fist, "Fire, we need fire. Do you have a spark?"

"Yeah, I have a lighter, it should work."

Kav moved off and started digging through the rubble, the furniture had been nice once, but most was worm-eaten now. It reminded him of a classroom, the way it was laid out, but there was truly no telling what purpose it had once served.

Liz watched him work, clutching the small silver lighter in her tiny fist. When he had built a suitable pile of wood he took the lighter to the downy stuffing and spongy wood at the bottom. It smelled awful but quickly took light, black smoke snaking its way up to the hole in the now dark skylight.

Kav squatted across from her, staring into the flames.

"If we find any longer sticks and good string we can make a splint for my leg, maybe even a crutch."

He nodded, only half listening to her.

"Kav?"

"What."

"Are you okay?"

"No"

"You want to talk? Seems we have nothing else to do." She looked down at herself and shrugged, pulling off the sodden jacket and shirts. She struggled with her pants for a moment but found she couldn't move enough with her leg throbbing, "A little help?"

Kav regarded her, wondering what to say before he stood and helped her ease out of the last of her soggy clothing. Her skin glowed pink in the firelight. Had he been human, he guessed this would be a distracting moment, but all he felt looking at her right now was mild curiosity and worry. In better circumstances he could appreciate the curiosity, but not right now.

"Thanks, I figured you wouldn't care if I took my crap off. It's all too wet and there is no better way to dry it right now."

She prodded it closer to the fire.

He was on his feet digging through the mess of furniture until he found enough parts to build a makeshift rack next to the fire. Setting her clothing on it, he dropped back to his place and rested his elbows on his knees.

She waited as he watched the fire, feeding it table legs now and then as the mud in his crest slowly dried and cracked.

"I don't know what to do now, Liz."

She nodded, her brows drawing together in sympathy.

"I.... I think I killed one of them, I pushed him over the railing. And why? Why were they there? What did they even want?" His whole body shook as his mind showed him the man floating down through the murky water, "I've never killed anyone, I've never seen a body, I've…"

Liz reached out and let her hand fall to her lap, "Kav, I don't know exactly what, but it sounded like they wanted you and your mother."

"My mother… she might be dead."

"If she is, these are the worst kidnappers in history."

Kav snorted, "Yeah, I guess you are right. I still have no idea what to do."

"We need rest, help me splint my leg and we can wait till morning and start walking south."

"But…"

Liz shook her head. "What other choice do we have?"

- 5 -

Kav had found the right sized sticks and some half-rotten fabric. Following her directions, he was able to make a workable shin splint. They sat up awake long enough for him to help her back into her mostly dry clothing. Most of the mud brushed away leaving stains on fabric and skin. Before long, the exhaustion had pressed them to the hard tile beside their makeshift fire.

An unknown time later, Kav's eyes snapped open. At first he couldn't tell what had woken him. The fire was down to low embers and Liz struggled with uneasy sleep across from him. Then he heard a faint clicking and the rattling of chain.

He bolted upright and earned a near miss of snapping jaws a hairs breadth away from his eyes. Kav scrambled back, scattering broken furniture. The massive grey-furred predator lunged and pulled short when the chain around its neck hauled it back.

Breathy laughter echoed around the chamber. The huge animal was hauled away from them as he huddled next to Liz. She clutched him, twining her fingers through his mud-caked crest.

Three figures stood shrouded in the gloom, their eyes reflecting the firelight in eerie shades of green. One by one, they stepped forward. Torn and patched clothing covered their bodies from head to toe. Heavy boots covered human-type feet, hoods and scarves obscured their faces. Only their eyes, huge and luminous, could be seen along with the paper white of the skin. Long, tangled crests of white hair hung out the backs of their hoods and goggles perched on top of their heads. Two were armed with primitive rifles, the third continued to reign in the monster that had almost torn his face off. It was almost big enough to ride yet it reluctantly obeyed its master.

Nilegi, as he had never seen them before, the normally clean aesthetics of their clothing long abandoned for reasons unknown.

One slung a rifle over his shoulder and squatted down at eye level next to Kav and Liz. The alien reached up and pulled down his scarves, revealing a paper white chin and swirling grey tattoos below his hugely dilated eyes.

"Ahn Aieloh?" His accent was thick with the syllabic hiss of his own tongue, "Wha you do here, Aieloh?"

"We were attacked. Humans attacked the humans at the tower."

"Tsst!" hissed the other gun-toting Nilegi, jerking her chin at the man. She, by her build anyway, started gesturing in the silent language of their kind. Hands flashed and Kav swallowed. They rarely taught the hand speak to outsiders so they always had a way to speak in private.

"What is going..." Liz grabbed his shoulders, readying herself to be scooped up at a run if it came to that

"Shh... wait," Kav watched them, his eyes tracking every movement.

The leader turned back to them, "Wha thesse humass do?"

"They wanted to kidnap me and my mother. We were there to work on the terraformer. That's all I know."

"Wha abou her?" he pointed to Liz.

Kav met the man's eyes, in the firelight the pale green of his iris was slowly contracting down, "They tried to kill her by throwing her to the storm, I dove after her."

The Nilegi smiled, a hissing laugh wormed its way out of him, "Youh! Dih youh thin sshe may-hate wih you?" His laughter infected the others, "Humas ah pihkey!"

Their laughter lost its hiss and the baritone notes of his voice bounced around the room. The man pulled off his gloves one by one, revealing the delicate white skin beneath, "Youh ah brave, Aieloh. Buh I doh beliehve youh."

His hands latched onto Kav's temples, he started to struggle but time seemed to bog down and make his already weary limbs heavier. A heat bloomed inside his head and the events of the past few weeks riffled past like the pages of a book blown by the wind. The heat increased and Kav could only clench his jaw against the pain. Then, as fast as it had started, it ended. The Nilegi was sitting back and rising to his feet while holding a palm to his forehead.

"Truh?" the woman shuffled forward but he waved her away as he tugged his gloves back on.

"Yess, you cohm with uss, Aieloh. You ahn youh wohman."

Their new captors laughed again as they nudged the two of them back to their feet, driving them deeper into the complex.

***

They wound through darkness, lumbering along before the snarling teeth of the guard animal and the Nilegi's probing gun barrels. The wind still screeched overhead and the rain drummed on, filling the passages with thunder. Another scream, muffled at first, started to raise and mingle with the keening storm.

"Wh…" Kav paused to ask and got shoved by the Nilegi for his question. It was so dark by now Kav couldn't see his hand in front of his face, but their captors were not so handicapped. Warm amber light seared his eyes when another metal door opened into a large room kept hot by many banked fires.

Blinking, he was shoved into the room. Kav tripped and stumbled to his knees. Liz yelped as she collapsed on her side. He went to her, hands on her face as he brushed her filthy red hair out of her eyes.

"I'm fine," Liz sat up and gazed open-mouthed around the room.

Two dozen Nilegi stood from their fires. Old men, children, and starved youths stared at them with eyes like obsidian — dark, hard, and sharp. All of them shared the same signs of desperation. Torn and patched clothing and wild, white dreadlocked hair hung long from the only strip where it grew in mohawks down their scalps. Most bore grey tattoos looping over cheeks and chins or even up along the edges of their long, tapered ears, but some, the young, did not. Hands flashed at their captors and signs were given back. The door was pressed closed just before another scream pierced the air. A woman's scream, the copper tang of blood, and the collected Nilegi's only reaction was to wince at the sound. Pieces were falling into place but not enough to make sense.

Kav pulled himself to his feet, "She, that woman, she's in labor? You brought a pregnant woman here? You're refugees aren't you? You snuck onto this planet! Do you have any idea how many council laws you are breaking by being here?"

"Shaut up!" The Nilegi who burned his mind before prepared a backhand.

"Why?" Kav flinched, but the strike never came.

With narrowed eyes, the man lowered his hand and looked away, "Yoh hav you'ar answer, Aieloh."

Kav blinked, letting the rest of the puzzle fall into place, "They are all like you? Psychics, you are all psychics!"

"Wait, like, mind reading?" Liz propped herself to her elbow, "Is that what happened back there?"

"Yes, and more. It all makes sense."

"Hold on, I'm still stuck on there being psychics. I mean, I heard rumors…"

The Nilegi hissed, "Youh humas cahnoh rea-ch Sana. Ask Aieloh friend. They cahn touch Sana same as we."

"Ok, but how does that makes sense? Why are you here?"

Kav leveled his gaze on their leader, "Because the Nilegi Imperium enslaves their psychics from birth. But not all of them want to be bound to the Ascendant or put into prison."

The man smirked, "Wha they say ahbou Aieloh is truh, youh ah clehvah."

"But to risk all, everything, to hide here?"

"Enough, I will speak to them now," a woman's hard-edged voice cut through the crowd.

Kav just noticed that the screaming had stopped.

All eyes trained to the far side of the room. She had stepped from behind a screen, head held high and a small bundle in her arms.

"You have checked their thoughts?" her accent was gratefully scant.

The man nodded and stepped away, she handed off her infant to him as she passed. The new mother sat next to Liz on the floor.

"Tell me why you are here, human and Ailo? Tell me how *Ori* has brought us together?"

"Ori? Is that a name? His name?" Liz nodded at the man.

The woman laughed, "No, although it should perhaps be *her* name." Her eyes settled on the bundle in her companions arms. She looked back at Liz the large lavender eyes boring into hers, "In your language it could mean fate. Now tell me, tell me why fate brings you to this storm-wrecked world?"

Kav shared a look with his red-haired friend and, with a shrug, he began.

***

Between them, Kav and Liz were able to recount the wild story that brought them here. Many inscrutable faces hardened when they got to the armed men invading the facility seeking Kav and his mother.

"How long?"

Kav blinked at her, "Dusk."

"Do you think they are still there?"

Kav gaped, he had no idea.

"It's possible the weather might keep them there," Liz had been given thin broth while they told their story and she sipped at it again, "or they might be in the air searching for us."

"Ori did bring us together, Ailo."

"Kav."

The woman smirked, "No names, you understand."

"Sorry, okay. Then help me understand what is going on here," he folded his arms.

The Nilegi woman nodded and showed him a rare smile, "Fine, I will indulge you. As you guessed, we came here to find a life free of our government. We are all psychic, each and every one of us. Not the mild psychic connections all of our people have, but truly awakened powers.

"We chose earth because of the human's lack of knowledge and its newness. So many places we could disappear. But the humans had other plans. These men who came to the tower, they are not normal mercenaries."

"Who are they then?" Liz murmured.

The woman glanced at her, "On Nis, I was all too familiar with their kind — special forces who work without public knowledge. Your people are hungry for psychic power and agents in your government wish to carry out experiments to wake the flame of *Sana* in your blood."

"Sana?"

The woman sighed, "There is no word I know... Soul? Essence? Power?" She shook her head, "The power to draw on the essence of life and impart your will on the cosmos."

"I think I get it," Liz shook her head, "But, no... no way we would risk conflict with aliens."

"Several of our group have already been taken by them. They do not consider us people. We are refugees, we do not exist. But..." she turned her eyes to Kav, "they want a larger sample. Tell me, Kav, are you and your mother...?"

"Psychic? I'm just a sensitive, but mother... she's a telepath."

"They will want you. A family line is even better for their research."

She stood and started directing her crew.

"Wait! What are you doing?"

"We hunt, our prey is in the tower."

Kav stood with her and grabbed her arm, "You are going after them? Shouldn't you be hiding?"

Her wide, lavender eyes settled on his hand, "Just because we understand the value of espionage does not make my people cowards. It is time we showed them we have teeth. We may not exist, but neither do these operatives. We will show them what it is to be ghosts."

Kav peeled his fingers from her arm, "But why?"

"Revenge, and as a warning to never harm my people again."

"I'm coming with you," the words jumped out of him before he could catch them.

The other Nilegi laughed. She grinned with a savage edge, "No, no, you are no warrior. You do not fight, that is not what you do."

Looking down at Liz, she added, "The old highway still sits above water, if you follow it south it should take you back to the embassies."

"My mother…"

"We will find her and free her. Beyond that, I make no promises. Go, take your human. Be gone from this place before we are."

He stared at his feet. They were right. Kav didn't know how to fight. It wasn't what he was good at, his mind was his tool and his will wasn't in fighting, in killing. He quivered like a leaf in the wind even thinking about a man he had simply pushed. What would outright murder do to him? It wasn't about physical strength, but he could no more fight than Liz could swim through turbulent water. Right now he knew a lot of things, the most important of which was that Liz needed help.

Eyes hard, he returned the woman's flinty gaze, "There are two ways in, a tunnel, and the platform. If they are expecting anything it will be on the platform. They won't know about the tunnel. It's a tight tunnel and full of heavy machinery. They will never hear you coming."

She nodded, "Thank you, we will remember."

"Please spare the humans who work there. They are just trying to save their world. They are the good ones. They are the ones worth saving."

He gazed down at Liz who smirked up at him. "Then you best go, Ailo."

Without another word, Kav scooped Liz into his arms and ducked back out the metal door as the sounds of battle preparation continued.

- 6 -

Thin dawn light found them picking along an empty highway, high winds threatening to blow them over every other moment. Kav carried her as long as he could, then let Liz limp until the pain was too much, Trading back and forth, they made their way up the highway. The only blessing they had was the moon. By its light alone they could see, when breaks in the clouds allowed shafts of silver to touch the city. Kav could see the blue orb gate in its round face when it bothered to seek them.

Silently, Kav bemoaned his rotten luck. He couldn't help but wonder if in some alternate dimension he was on the crew of Promise cruising to a distant colony instead of trudging along on this dense little planet, slogging through puddles on next to no sleep. All he wanted was a hot meal and a soft bed, he had had quite enough of this adventure.

Knowing luck was a perceptual thing did nothing for his mood. Fate, or the Makers, or Ori or whatever you wanted to call it, had nothing to do with it. Things just happened. Still, he couldn't be too hard on himself. The desire to make sense of the senseless was the hallmark of sentience, that simple curiosity that lead to discovery. The only pitfall was to always believe you had the final answer. *Final answer... final answer...* he could almost feel the revelation snapping into place.

He paused to stare at the sky. The storm was not done, but the sky was gradually clearing, leaving them exposed on the highway. Glancing at Liz, he realized it would be impossible to seek cover in the ruins. Between mudslides, debris, and Liz's swollen leg, that option was out of the question. Full understanding rocked him back on his heels.

Liz hobbled around in front of him on her makeshift crutch, "What is it? Why do you keep watching the sky?"

"They never went to the tower..."

"What? You mean the Nilegi? Why wouldn't they? They seemed pretty pissed..."

Kav had to admire her brains as he watched understanding blossom across her face, "Unless they had bait."

"Unless they had bait."

They both froze, like prey that had just caught scent of their own doom. High keening over the sigh of the wind told them what they already knew — a grav ship was heading their way.

Kav twisted his serpentine neck. They were high over the city, a veritable platter served up for their pursuers. Abandoned towers loomed nearby. Vacant windows stared back at them, helpless to avert their gaze from what was coming.

He shuffled in a circle, seeking any escape imaginable. The ship was visible now, angling at them from the north.

"What do we do?" Liz's eyes were ringed in white.

"I don't know. Nothing, play our part, I can't... Liz, they will kill you."

"I know, Kav."

He turned back to her, she dropped the crutch and limped over to him, wrapping her arms around his waist. Her head rested against his ribs, "Thank you for everything, even if it's all been for nothing. It's been a wonder to know you,"

Kav worked his jaw, trying to say something, anything, but opted instead to just wrap her up in his spindly arms.

The ship glided overhead and landed on the highway a short distance ahead. The engines settled and all sound vanished in the voice of the storm.

With a hiss, the back hatch opened and the same armed men from before filed out onto the concrete. Now in the light of day, he could see the fine equipment and healthy builds of trained men. Not mercenaries, not refugees seeking fortune. Soldiers.

"Did we interrupt something?" Their leader smirked at them, "Hey, fellas, should we catch this on film? How much do you think someone would pay for that?"

Laughter, ugly, shallow laughter.

Kav felt his pulse quicken for what he was about to do.

"Go," he whispered to her.

Before she could respond, he shoved her behind himself as he took a step forward.

"You will have to kill me to have her! It's me you want isn't it?"

The hiss came naturally, so too did the bristling crest, hands wide, claws displayed, tail lashing, primal posturing from millions of years of evolution. Several of the humans balked, buying him all the moment he needed.

He dove into them, head down and arms wide to catch as many as he could in his long limbs. Several went down with him before they could get their guns up. He rolled, grabbed a gun from another as they started to sight him and bat swung the soldier over the head.

Kav froze, staring at the bloody gun stock in his fist. Did he just kill a man? He looked up into the eyes of the next human as a gun barrel rose between them. Kav squeezed his eyes shut and jolted as the sound of gunfire thundered around him.

It all happened in heartbeats. When he opened his eyes again, the man lay dead and chaos reigned around him. Shots were coming from all around them, from the staring empty eyes of the buildings, from nearby rooftops, and from the crumbled debris behind them. The Nilegi had finally sprung their trap and they delivered promised punishment. One man ignited out of nowhere only to fall onto the wet pavement, sending up a plume of greasy black smoke. Another managed to scream "Ambush!" before a shot lanced his skull and dropped him to the ground. The remaining humans fired back, not caring who they struck.

"Liz!"

He bolted to where she cowered next to a pile of rubble.

Pain exploded in his side and he tumbled to the concrete. Somewhere he heard Liz scream. Crawling the rest of the way, he found Liz through the blinding pain and wrapped himself around her.

She struggled in his arms, but he held on as if she was all there was left of the world.

"Shhh, I got you. It's going to be okay."

The screams of dying men followed him into darkness.

***

Sound and sensation slowly leaked through the walls of his black prison. Dreams of future vistas and a green Earth haunted him, dreams of Promise and wishes unfulfilled. The voices came first, although their structure held no meaning. Then the voices crystalized into words. Someone was holding his hand.

"Kav? Come on, Kav," a woman, the words strangled as she spoke. Liz?

"My son, please, don't leave me. So young…" his mother sang to him as she spoke their native tongue.

He tried to respond but could only muster a gurgling wheeze, everything hurt, absolutely everything.

"He's alive!"

Motion all around him that he couldn't track. Hands pressed his side and warmth spread out from the wound like heat of the sun. Kav felt his body shudder and his exhausted muscles flexed and twitched.

When his eyes fluttered open, faces rayed around him — human, Ailo, Nilegi. Concern etched across their features. As he sat up, a young Nilegi shuffled away from his side to join the others. He sagged into another young woman's arms, completely exhausted. A crowd had gathered on the highway, the Nilegi and the humans from the terraformer. He couldn't remember feeling so grateful in his life. And when Kav looked down to the wound in his ribs he found it completely sealed, if a bit raw — a miracle, but not quite.

"A biokinetic" he breathed, "They are the rarest."

"We know," the Nilegi leader stepped into view as she slung a rifle over her shoulder, "that is why we hide, and why we must go. We have kept our promise. Find your path, friend Ailo, and walk it well."

She turned away.

"Wait!" Liz stood on her good leg, keeping balance against Telas. "What will you do now?"

The woman turned back. The dark lenses of her goggles rendered her expression unreadable, "Survive."

"But what about us? They may have gone about it wrong, but humans do need psychics. One of you lit that guy on fire. And Kav… you just saved his life. We need that. I mean, you could volunteer? Maybe they would take care of you?"

Silence to go with the black lenses. She turned away and watched the shuffling clouds, "You don't need us. Your people already have it. Just like all life has it. In time, I hope you will find it. On your own, without us. Trust me, you do not want to be in debt to my people."

There was a sigh on the wind, hauntingly beautiful as it touched broken pipes and hollows somewhere nearby. The Nilegi cocked her head to the side to listen to its notes.

Without another word, the ragtag collection of Nilegi boarded the grav ship and lifted off into the air.

Liz and the other humans waved and Telas mimicked the gesture as Kav found his feet.

He watched it fly to the north and felt his stomach sink.

"Hey, Mother, Liz, everyone — Umm… there went our ride…"

Liz stopped waving, "Oh, dammit."

***

A day later, their weary troop stumbled into the edge of the temporary city in the hills. Locals gawked at them and news spread fast that aliens had walked into town from a direction they shouldn't be. It wasn't long before authorities scooped them up and brought them back to what passed for a hospital.

They were treated for everything — dehydration, exhaustion, and a smattering of minor wounds, otherwise showing no major marks for their ordeal. The doctors wondered over his long healed bullet wound but asked no questions.

Kav dozed, grateful to even be alive, and by morning found himself enjoying a blue sky through his windows when Liz came limping in on a set of real crutches.

"Are you even supposed to be up?"

Liz looked much better, no more mud dulling her fire red hair, no more darkness under her eyes.

"They said I could hop around this floor."

"So you came to see me?"

"Of course," Liz hobbled over to his bedside and plopped her rump next to his knees, "you saved my life, twice! You are the first person I came to see."

"Eh," Kav shrugged it off.

"Shut up, I have things to say. You are brave, I don't care what the Nilegi said."

He snorted, "It was stupid, I was afraid."

"Bravery *is* stupid, and you wouldn't be sane if that didn't scare the crap out of you."

Kav nodded as they lapsed into silence.

When she spoke again her voice was soft as a feather, "What are we going to tell them, Kav?"

He shrugged, "Let my mother take care of it, she will know what to say and they won't hound her for the truth."

"No problem. Say, by the way, I had a friend go and get you something."

Liz fished into the pocket of her hospital gown. Her tiny fist came out concealing whatever she had. Kav leaned forward in anticipation.

"What is it?"

"Hold out your hand and close your eyes."

"Okay," he did as instructed and was rewarded with a smooth, heavy, cool sphere in his outstretched palm.

"Ok, open your eyes."

Whatever human custom he just engaged in, he liked it very much. When he opened his eyes, he caught his breath. A perfect glass orb rested in his hand, the surface swirling deep blue and dots of green. His home captured in perfect miniature as if his hands were the universe.

"It's Susite, I figured you would..."

Kav wrapped her in a hug, "Thank you, it's beautiful."

Laughing, she sat back and patted his knee, "Once they let us out of here you want to go, I dunno, have a beer? Watch a movie or something? I could use a friend after all this madness."

He felt his crest poof at being called a friend, "You sure they would let me do that?"

"Pfft… I don't think they could argue with the hero who saved the Earth Renew Project."

"Hero? I like that."

"Heh, well, don't like it too much, it's a little hazardous."

"I might just settle for being a hero only once."

They laughed, her throaty chuckle, his bark, they sounded different but the sentiment was universal.

"Promise me something, Kav"

"What? Anything."

She looked up at him, tears lining her eyes, "When I'm long gone and you live on, come back to my world, see the work we have done, and remember me."

Kav leaned forward and rested his forehead on hers, "I promise. As certain an oath as I made on my graduation day."

Liz pressed her lips to his cheek and ruffled his crest before her laughter broke through like shafts of sunlight. He felt what she did, hope, hope for a better world as promising as her laughter and the rays of light after a storm.

***

Dawn in his salvage shop, Kav shuddered as all of it flooded back to him in the blink of an eye. Memories two hundred years distant bubbled up as he gazed into the smooth surface of the blown glass in his palm.

Over time a city had grown around that half remembered cluster of prefab buildings where his feet had first touched the Earth. It was a city Liz could not have imagined for her world. New Byzantia shimmered as a jewel of the new cities, a wonder of technology and a multicultural hub touched by the galaxy. And now it was his home.

Kav let his eyes smile as he remembered Liz VanVeen, the red-haired human who had been his first true friend. She might be gone, but her legacy lived on in a world made green again. Even as the world had changed around him, Kav had kept his promise, he remembered, and he endured and, again, he would do something stupid to be a hero.

The End